Words & Music by Pete Seeger   Paintings by Linda Wingerter

One Grain of Sand

A Lullaby

Megan Tingley Books
LITTLE, BROWN AND COMPANY
New York ♂ An AOL Time Warner Company

1837

Also by Pete Seeger:

Abiyoyo®
Abiyoyo Returns®
Pete Seeger's Storytelling Book

To Tinya Seeger
—P. S.

For Sam
—L. W.

First Edition

Library of Congress Cataloging-in-Publication Data

Seeger, Pete.
    One grain of sand : a lullaby / words and music by Pete Seeger ; paintings by Linda
Wingerter.— 1st ed.
        p.   cm.
    Summary: A lullaby celebrating the fragility of the environment, the innocence
of childhood, and the sense that we all are connected and part of the world's family.
    ISBN 0-316-78140-1
    1. Lullabies, American—Texts.   2. Folk songs, English—United States—Texts.
[I. Lullabies. 2. Folk songs—United States.]   I. Wingerter, Linda S., ill.   II. Title.
PZ8.3.S4505 On 2002
782.42'1582—dc21
[E]   00-050687

10 9 8 7 6 5 4 3 2 1

MON

Printed in Spain

The illustrations for this book were done in acrylics on bristol board.
The text was set in Diotima Roman, and the display type is Reckleman Script.

A Note from the Songwriter

Dear Readers and Singers,

What an honor to see my little song so beautifully illustrated! This song started to take shape in 1956, when our youngest child, Tinya, was less than a year old. Over the next months and years, verses and melodies were improvised. It's been recorded by Odetta as well as by other singers; and in August 2000 I heard a rock band do it.

    I hope anyone holding this book will also sometime hold a baby or small child. Don't be afraid of changing words or repeating words. Change the melody if you want. We have many, many traditions of lullabies in this country. You may know melodies that I would never think of. Here's the one I usually use:

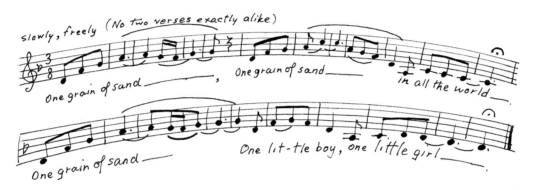

Sometimes the last line is longer; in this case, you can repeat a musical phrase, as here:

Some of the most successful singing I've ever done has been when one hundred percent of my audience has gone sound to sleep on me.

Yours for more homemade music,

Pete Seeger
Beacon, New York

Pete and Tinya

One grain of sand,
One grain of sand in all the world,
One grain of sand,
One little boy, one little girl.

One grain of sand,
One lonely star up in the blue,
One grain of sand,
One little me, one little you.

One grain of sand,
One drop of water in the sea,
One grain of sand,
One little you, one little me.

One grain of sand,
One little snowflake lost in the swirling storm,
One grain of sand,
I'll hold you close to keep you warm.

One grain of sand,
One leaf of grass upon a plain,
One grain of sand,
I'll sing it now again and again and again.

One grain of sand,
One grain of sand in all the world,
One grain of sand,
One little boy, one little girl.

One grain of sand,
One grain of sand is all my joy,
One grain of sand,
One little girl, one little boy.

One grain of sand,
One little raindrop splashed into my eye,
One grain of sand,
One little you, one little I.

One grain of sand,
One little snowflake lost in the swirling storm,
One grain of sand,
I'll hold you close to keep you warm.

One grain of sand,
One leaf of grass upon a plain,
One grain of sand,
I'll sing it now again and again and again.

One leaf of grass,
One leaf of grass on a windy plain,
One leaf of grass,
We come and go again and again.

The sun will rise,
The sun will rise and then go down,
The sun will rise,
One little world goes round and round
 and round.

So close your eyes,
So close your eyes and go to sleep,
So close your eyes,
One little smile, one little weep.

One grain of sand,
One grain of sand upon the shore,
One grain of sand,
One little life, who'd ask for more?

One grain of sand,
One drop of water in the sea,
One grain of sand,
One little you, one little me.

One grain of sand,
One grain of sand is all my own,
One grain of sand,
One grain of sand is home sweet home.

So go to sleep,
So go to sleep by the endless sea,
So go to sleep,
I'll hold you close, so close to me.

One grain of sand,
One grain of sand in all the world,
One grain of sand,

One little boy, one little girl.